DAPHNE

Author: Aphrodite Mermiga-Vlachaki
Translator: Irene Angelidou
Cover designer: Stavros Vlachakis
Production supervisor: Platon Malliagkas
www.mediterrabooks.com

ISBN 978-960-93-7472-9

Aphrodite Mermiga-Vlachaki

DAPHNE

A novella

AV

It is strange to dream, and to have mirrors
Where the commonplace, worn-out repertory
Of every day may include the illusory
Profound globe that reflections scheme.

Jorge Luis Borges

To those who dream

CONTENTS

The opening chords of the piano sound like wistful bells in the crowded concert hall. A deep, intense feeling engulfed her as the orchestral part rolled in.

Tonight, the Athenian audience is enjoying a special evening. One of the harshest music critics, with a regular column in the Greek newspaper *Kathimerini*[1], is sitting in one of the front rows and is following the tempo of the music with his right foot, his eyes trained on the ceiling.

At the podium, one of the most famous conductors, a student of the composer himself.

At the piano, he, Daniel Andremont.

---

1 Famous daily morning newspaper published in Athens since 1919.

Part One

Moderato

They were very close when they were young. Angela, the oldest – though they were only a year apart – with the dark brown hair and eyes, was sociable and open.

Daphne, the little one – as they often called her – was fair and reserved.

Growing up, they complemented each other. And when the time came to decide on their future, they did the same. The eldest one left to study in France while the young one stayed behind, content in her household responsibilities and social engagements.

Besides, theirs was an affluent family. Nonetheless, the oldest one didn't possess a grain of sense, their old grandmother would say, with that look in her eyes that made them quake in their boots when they were children. The eyes of their father's mother, the descendant of a family that had produced several leaders of the Greek War of Independence of 1821, still blazed with fire even though she was well over eighty.

The youngest member of the family, cheerful but taciturn, a disposition similar to moderato, followed faithfully in her mother's footsteps.

The moment she finished her education, and had mastered the French language – both sisters had a French teacher from as far back as they could remember – and piano lessons – as many as necessary, she dived into her social life. That meant tea parties, charity events, balls, and gowns for all these events; and of course, there was the cinema, the theatre, and concerts as well.

However, she had something that made her stand out from other girls her age. Her love for literature, or rather... her passion.

Her room was filled with books. And since its old-fashioned décor didn't allow her to have her own bookcase, all of her books were stacked in piles around the room, even on the floor right next to her bed. In vain did Dina, who cleaned their house three times a week, try to make sense of the young lady's fascination with books...

Novels were her favourite. Particularly those of French and Russian writers and poets; she read the latter from French translations. Lately, she had discovered a Greek poet from Alexandria, the one called Constantine P. Cavafy, who had enchanted her with his style and unique poetic language. Her father though – they would discuss the intellectual life of Athens after dinner – who was faithful to the Athenian school and its more traditional style of poetry, had a different opinion.

And, thus, the poet became all hers in her solitary hours.

'Hurry up. Everyone has gathered in the living room,' Dina whispered to her, poking her head with the bushy fiery-blonde hair into the room.

The girl threw a brief glance at her three-door wardrobe mirror, let out a nervous sigh and, after turning off the lights of her room as she had been taught to do since childhood, she stepped out onto the landing.

Everything looked festive in the entrance hall. The two large chandeliers illuminated the interior with their rich light. The glass dividing doors between the living and the dining room were wide open.

The oval dining table, set with the white linen tablecloth with dainty stitching in the corners; the crisp, matching napkins, artfully placed on the white Rosenthal plates; the silver cutlery and the crystal glasses of varying sizes, some for water, some for wine; the two Chinese vases with the white orchids – a gift from the hostess' cousin, the one who had sailed the distant seas for years – one placed on the corner table and the other on the sideboard...

Everything set to mark the evening's special occasion in the year 193...

Their two guests were sitting comfortably in a pair of 18th century Louis XIV (or was it XV?) armchairs – which had been part of the hostess' dowry. It was Mrs. Georgiou, née Anagnostopoulou, a widow, and her son, Alexandros Georgiou. Her son, newly arrived from Paris, was a doctor, a lung specialist, a specialty that was very popular in the medical circles of their time.

Mrs. Georgiou was the widow of a statesman belonging to Venizelos' Liberal Party[2]. Twice he had been a parliamentary candidate for some prefecture in Central Greece and twice he had failed. When he suddenly died from gastrorrhagia in the 1920s, everybody was taken aback. They couldn't accept the sudden passing of gentle Mr. Anastasis.

His wife, broken-hearted over the loss of her husband, found consolation in the correspondence she kept with her son, who had just left

---

2 Political party founded in 1910 by Eleftherios Venizelos, who served seven times as Greek Prime Minister.

for the French capital in order to pursue his specialty.

Since then, mother and son developed a special bond with each other.

The melody, so graceful and yet so stately, so tuneful but also so delicate, made her shiver. The notes from the piano awakened unexpected feelings in her soul.

Daphne slowly – if a bit reluctantly – went down the staircase that led to the entrance hall and passed through the double doors, which were also festively open towards the living room, with princess-like grace.

Lively voices sounded in her ears. She looked to the right and saw her father's smiling face, and her mother standing by his side, resplendent in her dark green velvet dress. She looked more beautiful than her daughter would have ever imagined.

Her habitually black-clad grandmother was sitting in the Viennese armchair, rocking back and forth as she was wont to do. Her gold cross necklace, a family heirloom from her great-grandmother, shone around her neck. A silver comb gleamed in her white hair. Daphne recalled that, many years ago, she had discovered it in a box hidden at the bottom drawer of her bedside table. Her grandmother had given her a severe scolding back then for riffling through her things without permission.

Tonight, it was quite the opposite. Her grandmother was smiling at her and her eyes held nothing of the severity that made Daphne feel apprehensive.

A discourse between the piano and the rest of the orchestra followed. A discourse between the soul and the absolute. An endless discourse that his fingers had initiated as they glided over the keys of the piano and carried her into a vortex of playful and bold tones. It was as if the piano stitched vibrant sounds between the stringed instruments. Everyone's eyes were fixed on the stage; they were almost breathless, swept away by the music...

Daphne greeted their guests politely and took the seat nearest to Mrs. Georgiou. Dina had just placed the silver tray with the rose petal sweet preserve on a side table. It was the hostess' specialty.

At first, they exchanged a few customary pleasantries. When they all sat around the dinner table a little later, the atmosphere had become warmer. Politics played a leading part in their conversation, after they had praised the delicious dishes prepared by their two hostesses, mother and daughter.

As if by coincidence, the two men, Alexandros and Daphne's father, found themselves agreeing wholeheartedly with each other on political issues. It is no small matter to share the same political views as your future son-in-law. You saved yourself from many troubles, especially heated arguments with unforeseen consequences.

Those years were troubled; politically unstable.

Europe had changed. It had lost the vibrant colours of its past. It was as though a dull greyness had spread throughout the continent. Everyone had entered a whirlpool which would be very difficult to escape from. Both pessimists and realists realized that. Her father was a staunch realist. He was well aware of it and so was Alexandros. It had quickly dawned on him too.

Alexandros, who had kept stealing glances at her all night long.

They had a detailed discussion about the prime minister's policy of the last five years, specifically praising his handling of foreign policy issues.

Then it was time to change the subject, her mother said with a hidden smile, and move on to lighter topics, which made the women enter a lively conversation – even Dina, who was stacking their empty dinner plates on a tray, shared her passionate opinion about the new role of women in society and the feminist movement. Mrs. Georgiou directly condemned those women who only cared about showing their naked calves, and Daphne's father agreed with her.

At the end of the evening, their guests were left with a pleasant feeling from the hours spent together in the living room of the Andreadis family. Each one for their own reasons.

The next day, at around eleven o' clock in the morning, the telephone's ring sounded throughout the house, even in the upstairs bedrooms.

She recalled how jubilant her mother's face looked as she placed the handset back in its cradle. As if someone had given her the sky.

Why did all these recollections of her personal history come back to the forefront of her mind after all these years, she thought, as she put her earrings back in the alabaster jewellery box, a gift from her sister on one of their visits to Paris.

A melody haunted her mind and she struggled to remember where it came from, but it was impossible.

Pace pace, mio Dio!

Once more, she saw him on the stage as he bowed to his adoring audience. Then, he gave a slight bow to the old conductor and walked confidently towards the piano. He raised the piano bench a touch and sat down. He moved his upper body back and forth to find the proper position, gently placed his hands on the piano keys in the complete silence of the auditorium, and sank into the nostalgia hidden in the music.

It was to be his only performance in front of the Athenian audience and then he would be off to perform in many major cities around the world.

He was Angela's, her sister's, great conquest. Her latest 'acquisition'. That was what Daphne somewhat bitterly thought when she received her sister's telegram a few days before.

Athens had not been part of his tour, but when his manager made a last-minute change in their schedule, they had unexpectedly ended up in Greece, her sister wrote in her too-long telegram.

'The little one...' Her sister's words ended in uncontrollable laughter, just as she remembered from the past.

'... Your sister-in-law, as we say here. It has been many years since you last met. N'est-ce pas, mon cher?'

'It's a figure of speech. I'm not so little anymore...' Daphne had answered with a smile.

His eyes sank into her eyes. Greyish-green and disarming...

Memory negates time by bringing the past into the present without distorting it.

It had been several years before, when she and her husband had found themselves in Paris for a few days, that she met him for the first time, in a haze of feelings and illusions. Alexandros had made some bitter comments about her sister, her new inamorato and her circle of friends that followed them at every step. The Parisian press had recently hailed her brother-in-law as the latest grand musical discovery and they were constantly in the limelight.

She only had a few vague and somewhat insignificant memories from those days. Then, a few years passed and so many things happened in the meantime that only the rare letter and the even rarer phone call kept those memories alive.

She ushered them into the living room and served them glasses of liqueur. They were in a hurry. They had to leave for the dress rehearsal. He was not usually late... unlike other soloists, Angela remarked as she stood at the front door. He was always punctual.

Her sister talked and talked incessantly.

He did not take his eyes off her...

Daphne did not have the chance to say much. Just that they would all be there the following evening. At the grand concert hall of the Rex Theatre[3].

---

3 One of the most important modern theatres in Athens. It was founded in 1937 and has been the main stage of the National Theatre of Greece since 1993.

It was about eight o' clock in the evening when the black limousines started arriving outside the Hotel Grande Bretagne one after the other. The night was dedicated to the three grand personas of the following day's concert. One of them, the composer, had already passed away a few years before. He had spent his last years in the fame and recognition that his divine talent had granted him.

In the magnificent reception hall of the aristocratic hotel, the other two honoured guests, the conductor and the pianist, were surrounded by music experts and enthusiasts.

His height and thick hair made him stand out in the crowd. Flushed from all the hugs and kisses he received, Daniel was smiling at everyone. Occasionally, after having slipped away from one of his admirers, he would glance right and left, as if he were looking for something.

At some point, his wife approached him, wrapped her arm around his waist and clung to him in a blatant manner. He stroked her hair as his eyes wandered over her head.

A group of middle-aged female admirers stole him somewhat awkwardly from her side.

The orchestra passionately started playing a gentle, harmonious melody. The piano followed, more melodious, and even more passionate.

Her eyes were fixed on him. She had lost all sense of time. Could it be that time had ceased to exist for her, lost as she was in moments of her own time, of her own present?

Shortly before the concert, as she was sitting in front of her dressing table mirror in the bedroom she shared with her husband, gently applying rouge on her paler than ever cheeks, she looked directly into the eyes of her reflection and twin pools of despair gazed back at her...

A spark, a tiny little spark seemed to spring from those eyes.

With an adept movement, she clasped her white pearl necklace behind her neck; it would be the only ornament on herself, except for her eyes.

As his admirers vied for his attention, he

searched for her eyes. At one point, he discovered them trained on him...

Their eyes met and there was an instant communion between their souls and their bodies.

She had her children with her tonight. He was the 'new uncle,' as they called him at home, but he became the 'lost uncle' later, when they learned things about him in the newspapers.

The children were all grown up now. Her boys, both of them true gentlemen, were the focal point of all the young girls present. Petros, her eldest son, had just become a doctor, and, at that time, he was completing his specialty training in Paris, just as his father had done before him; her youngest son, Costas, was in his last year of law school. As for her daughter, twenty-year-old Vasia, a student at the Marasleio Academy of Education, she was so different from her brothers, so different from her mother.

She so resembled Angela! As if she were her

sister's daughter and not her own, she thought with a touch of disappointment but also with a deep, secret joy.

Daphne looked at her daughter in admiration as Vasia became the centre of attention of their present company.

It had been three years since Alexandros' death and the concert was the occasion where the family was once again becoming part of Athenian social life.

She was alone in her bedroom, in the complete darkness that she had got used to, her head buried in her feather pillow as her open eyes gazed into the black nothingness, into the bottomless depths of her mind where scenes from the past, present and possible future intermingled and smothered her.

She reached for the crystal water glass that she always placed on her bedside table from when she was a girl, in case she grew thirsty. Now, how much she needs this water! To quench the thirst born of the unspeakable thoughts hidden deep within the fathomless and forbidding night of her soul.

The moonlight just barely entered through

the window grilles, shedding a faint light on her feet.

The image of her sister as she had been at the reception just a few hours ago. Carefree, and at the same time insecure, laughing, and alternately holding a cigarette or a half-filled glass of whiskey in her right hand. She had found Daphne much changed, she said; yet, hadn't she changed as well? It was as if Angela had lost some of her self-assurance.

She panicked. She had just touched the chord of a memory, and she immediately banished it, just like a discordant melody, an off-key note.

And then the image of her older sister reappeared behind the crystal glass, the half-filled glass, with her face distorted.

And, once more, she heard that melody, which she couldn't for the life of her name.

Idle chatter, hugs, laughter, the clinking of cutlery and glass in the hands of the guests, and light. The light of the chandeliers was

everywhere. And a distorted face laughing behind a crystal glass half-filled with whiskey.

And eyes everywhere. A room filled with
eyes.

His eyes.

Fortunately, her daughter approached her.
How she prattled!

Ah, the French language! She hadn't used
it in years.

Just browsed through a French magazine
from time to time.

Vasia interrogated him outright. She was filled with pride as she listened to her daughter speak a foreign language so fluently, as though it were her mother tongue. He answered her questions patiently. His eyes, though, were constantly fixed on Daphne.

Her cheeks grew hot every time she felt his gaze on her. She got incredibly angry at his audacity, but not for long.

She suddenly felt that she needed to get away. To retire to her bedroom. To find refuge in her solitude and her chaotic reveries.

But, it was impossible. The night was far from over.

These people were her family and friends.

The guest of honour was her brother-in-law. She couldn't just slip away. What would people think?

What would Angela think?

And his eyes followed her, no matter where she stood in the room. This game couldn't go on any longer.

But, what if it didn't?

She was alone in her bedroom, in the complete darkness that she had got used to, her head buried in her feather pillow as her open eyes gazed into the black nothingness.

Her sister. After spending so many years apart, they had forgotten how to look each other in the eye. They just looked at each other. Angela would sometimes observe her younger sister and then she would just burst out into that laugh Daphne knew so well from the past. Only now, it was as though her sister was trying to hide something behind her laughter.

Her mind kept replaying her sister's distorted face through the half-filled glass of whiskey as she placed her own water glass on the bedside table.

Suddenly, she became agitated.

Her sister's life unravelled in Daphne's mind like a silent film where the actors have no voice and the plotline can be summarized in a few sentences.

The most important ones.

She had been married twice – this was her second marriage – and she had no children from either of her husbands.

'Children are a commitment,' Angela had told her several times, in the dusk of their girlish dreams.

There were times when Daphne would wake up in the middle of the night to find her older sister still awake. The small night light, which their parents used to leave turned on in the corridor in order to calm their fear of the dark, played upon her form as she lay on the bed, with her hands folded behind her head, her eyes wide open. She dreamt of living a life different from her own. A life beyond conventions, a life of her own, where she would follow her own rules.

And once more, Daphne remembered her sister's distorted face, the way she had seen it at the reception, through that glass of whiskey.

Part Two

Adagio sostenuto

Once more, the strings join the rest of the orchestra. Then the flute, the oboe, and the clarinet. The melody is so lyrical, filled with nostalgia for everything she has lived and everything she hasn't. And he, slightly leaning towards the piano, is accompanying the woodwinds, while slowly initiating a new discourse with her. With her soul...

It was just yesterday, a bit before noon, at the beach of Faliro, where the waves met the sand. He had approached her when they found themselves a bit further away from the rest of their group. He called her Laura[4]. She remembered her student years. Her beloved teacher! That was the last time anyone had called her by that nickname. She felt his touch on her shoulders but she kept her composure. As if she had been expecting it.

She had taken her shoes off and was letting the seawater cool her toes, just as she used to do when she was a child.

---

4 Feminine version of the Latin name Laurus, which means 'laurel'. Daphne also means 'laurel' in Greek.

'Laura! Laura!'
And then the calmness that follows distant memories. An eternity that lasts for a moment. Her sister was a few feet away from them, sitting at a big table covered with a checked tablecloth, chatting with Daphne's children, and their friends.

Angela had earned her degree in History of Art and had specialized in *Art Contemporain* – one of the few women to graduate from a male-dominated field of study – but public relations was what she loved and what suited her best. She attended seminars, lectures and concerts. A group of like-minded people formed around her and they would regularly gather for discussions and debates in a café in the Rive Gauche much frequented by intellectuals.

She met her first husband by moving in these social circles. He was a Greek intellectual with many useful connections who opened many doors for his new wife. They had a whirlwind romance that quickly fizzled out.

One day, Angela just opened the door of their house and left because, she said, she couldn't deal with that kind of commitment any more. It was that simple to her.

Luckily, their father never found out about the divorce. He had passed away content in the knowledge that his eldest daughter had got married at last, even if it was in a foreign country.

Fatalità! Fatalità! Fatalità!

D aphne feels the force embracing her as she loses herself in the nostalgia of the music born of those hands... A powerful, invincible force, something like fate when it interferes in the life of someone seeking happiness... Would it have been better if she had just turned her back on reality and allowed herself to sink into her dreams? To smother her soul in those dreams...

Her sister is looking at her straight in the eyes through the crystal. A tear is shining in the corner of her eye. Or is it not a tear?

Their trip to Faliro was her sister's idea. Perhaps she felt nostalgic for the past. When they were young, they would travel to the seaside with their parents and cousins on every sunny, winter Sunday. Angela rarely stayed with their group. She would sit further away, at the place where the waves met the sand, and she would play with the small pebbles, lost in her reveries.

These memories were probably what made her suggest this outing yesterday, after so many years and so many unexpected events. Besides, her sister said in an attempt to make them share her enthusiasm, it was no longer a journey, as in the past, but just a short drive.

Daphne felt somewhat uncomfortable as she sat in the front passenger seat, next to her son,

Petros, who was their driver. Her brother-in-law was sitting in the back, right behind the driver's seat; his eyes pinned on her profile. Her sister and his manager – who never left the married couple's side – were sitting in the back with him. He was humming a popular song that was playing on the radio, while Petros was enjoying the thrill of speeding along a nearly empty highway which led to the seaside.

Angela was chattering non-stop, as always, but the rest of their group was clearly not in the mood to indulge her. Petros kept waving to his brother, who was following them in a black sedan, with Vasia in the co-driver's seat.

She was alone in her bedroom, in the complete darkness that she had got used to – so much so that she didn't complain about it anymore – her eyes gazing into the black nothingness as she sinks into unprecedented depths with no bottom in sight...

'Oh, Father! You muttered her name just before you left us, just before I lowered your eyelids.'

She sat up in the dark, frightened.

The fingerboard of memory once again ...

'Only God and I know the secrets of my soul.' This too she had read somewhere. Why couldn't she remember where?

Fate gave her a rough awakening. Like the sword of Damocles, it hung over her head, powerful and inescapable. She felt her loneliness even more sharply.

A sweet, tender dream embraced her for a moment. She had ceased to exist, and so had all the others. Anything that might have been dark and joyless had ceased to exist... Even if only for a moment.

And, afterwards, the same off-key note, the crystals, the distorted face. The sound of a short, vain laugh. Her splintered past. And, afterwards, the calmness that follows distant memories.

She got up and turned on the light. She let it flood the room. Her wedding picture was standing on her small bedside table; unmoving, silent and inexorable. She instinctively stood up and abruptly turned it the other way.

And, once more, that melody that kept haunting her mind.

The faint silhouette of the island of Aegina appeared in the distance. They were on a bright red boat with its sails wrapped around the mast, its colour in sharp contrast to the blue and white hues of the Saronic Gulf. The rest of their group, just a few feet away from them, were chatting incessantly amongst themselves. Among the general clamour, her sister's bubbly laugh stood out just like when they were children.

He took her hand in his. She abruptly pulled it away, but immediately regretted it. She tried to steal a glance at him and saw that his gaze was on her. She lowered her head and had to use all her strength in order to keep herself from looking directly at him. It was as if she were struggling against an unseen force.

She felt uncomfortable and guilty.

Let not this moment end, dear Lord. Let it last for eternity.

His left hand enters a new discourse with the woodwind section, which conveyed her to different places, and undiscovered paths.

He reaches the cadenza, with his eyes half-shut, and she is swept away by a stream of pain.

Her life was a painting, just like one of those paintings she saw and admired in the various European museums she had visited in the first years of her marriage when she would accompany Alexandros to conferences.

'Don't let your husband go alone. You should go with him,' her mother had told her with a meaningful wink the first time Alexandros was to attend a conference in Brussels.

'Men are shallow and never stop chasing skirts,' Dina had added, for she had spent half her life as the wife of an unfaithful man.

Her life was a painting, like one of those Flemish paintings depicting the contented families of 17th century Calvinist society. It was as if whimsical Vermeer, from the faraway city of Delft, had painted their family portrait. Alexandros, with an ambitious, haughty look in his eyes and a faint smile on his lips, and Daphne standing solemnly by his side, with an acquiescent look on her beautiful face, radiating youth, her hand resting gently on the head of her youngest son, who is trying to appear equally solemn, standing next to his brother and his little sister.

And the painting would be mounted in an impressive gold-gilded frame, just like those decorating the reception hall in the Hotel Grand Bretagne, the place where his eyes kept seeking hers a few hours earlier.

In the darkness of her bedroom – just a few moments earlier she had turned over their wedding photo on her bedside table – she recalled the day Alexandros asked for her hand in marriage. The scene passed through her mind with lightning speed, but she didn't try to expel it.

She had felt so wonderful at the thought that more colour would be added to her life, that it would change.

It wasn't that she hadn't been content living in her family home. But everything changed when one morning she saw her father, who had just entered the house with a newspaper under his arm, as was his habit, looking worn

out, burdened by the many years of his life —
how hadn't she noticed it before? And, then,
Alexandros appeared, filled with dreams and
ambitions, carrying her away into a bright future. She knew what she had to do.

She took the decision sound of heart and
mind. Mostly, sound of mind.

Besides, at that time, two of her closest
friends had also got married, one shortly after
the other.

It was as if the three of them had won the
same bet.

And, then, as if by magic, the faces in the
painting, still in the same positions, change ex-
pressions. A few years have gone by. The three
children are older. The boys have neat haircuts
and are dressed formally. The girl has long,
blond hair and is wearing a form-fitting skirt
which subtly accentuates her emerging womanly figure.

And, then, there are the parents. The father
has thinning hair, but his eyes have gained

wisdom, and Daphne herself appears older, but perhaps more beautiful, with the same acquiescent expression in her eyes.

Twenty years of her life. Twenty years of her life in a single painting, just like those in the Hotel Grand Bretagne. With the impressive gold-gilded frames.

And Daphne, within a futile life dream, which today, just a few hours ago, she felt sinking beneath her feet...

The next morning, she woke up with a headache. Her head was throbbing. For a moment, she felt frightened. She slowly went down the stairs and entered the kitchen in order to take a painkiller for her headache. She swallowed it at once. It was so quiet around her, as if no one else was in the house. She hadn't even checked the time.

She made her way to the living room where her life had changed so many years ago. The large clock on the wall read nine o'clock. But her eyes turned to the large dining table and, for a moment, her mind travelled to the past. She cradled her forehead in her hands.

The pill still hadn't taken effect. Oh, God! No more thoughts.

She rushed out of the living room and flew up the stairs. She made it to the middle of the staircase where she made a short pause to catch her breath.

For two days, she had been living in a whirlwind. She just realized that it had swept her away... If her father were still alive...

She climbed up the remaining steps. *Everyone must have left*, she thought. Then, she remembered everybody's schedule. And the painkiller finally gave her some relief.

Daphne had arranged to meet her children at seven o' clock tomorrow afternoon so that they could all go to The Pantheon, a restaurant. To the official farewell dinner.

This is where it ended.

In the privacy of her bedroom, she cast one more look at her reflection in the mirror, the same thing she had done a few hours ago with secret womanly pride.

A few hours ago, his eyes had been seeking her face among so many others. A few hours ago, his hands had touched her soul. A few hours ago, Angela had given her that strange look and, afterwards, had let out that familiar laugh.

The outing to Faliro had been yesterday morning.

Those few hours suddenly seemed an eternity.

They had grown too far apart. Angela hadn't stood still long enough for them to talk like sisters do, or have a chat about the old days, which seemed so far away now. She was unsure if Angela remembered anything at all from her life in Greece. So many years had passed, and there had also been a war.

Angela in Paris. Angela in New York. Angela had been to so many places. Daphne had spent all of her holidays in Greece. On rare occasions, and once for a whole winter – that horrible winter during the German Occupation – they had stayed at her uncle's farm in a small rural town in the Peloponnese.

Why is she stirring things up so late at night?

And Angela, whom she hadn't seen for so long... So distant, practically a stranger.

The look she had given her yesterday...

How she misses everyone this morning. Not the living. It was fortunate that they were away at the moment. She didn't wish to be observed.

Her daughter would have instantly noticed that something was wrong with her mother.

Alexandros' photograph was staring at her from the corner of the sideboard. He had a languid look in his eyes, exactly like her life had been after she married him. She knew of his many infidelities, but she had turned a blind eye to them. That was the proper thing to do. She couldn't ruin her family over such 'insignificant' matters. It was how she had been brought up.

Besides, habit has a way of regulating everything.

The 'other woman' was a doctor. An ambitious careerist, as became apparent in retrospect. Daphne had even met her once, at a social event held in one of the grand hotels in Athens.

She glanced furtively at her husband's photograph. Had these events been part of her own life, she wondered, or had she read them in some book?

Her children had been so young back then. Her oldest son was just ten years old. She instantly recalled how many tears she had shed. If she had been the one shedding them...

Why did she suddenly remember all of these things?

She had buried the 'incident' deep inside her mind and it had now decided to dig its way up to the surface. Now that everything in her life had turned upside down. What life? Did she ever have a life of her own?

Perhaps she was losing her mind.

'A woman has to live for others, not for

herself.' She knew her lesson by heart. This is what she had witnessed happening in her house, ever since she was a little girl.

But, not Angela. She had never learned her lesson.

What to wear? She hadn't even thought about it.

She opened her large wardrobe. Her clothes, all crammed together before her, seemed insufficient, just like when she was a young girl getting ready for a grand night out. *Nothing changes*, she thought... She would wear the same dress she had worn at the reception. She had no desire to dwell on the matter any longer. Why should she torture herself?

In a few hours, everything would be over. What would be over?

After the concert, they all gathered for a farewell dinner at The Pantheon in Stadiou Street.

Laughing faces, best wishes and congratulatory words in every language. Elegant young people, middle-aged ladies, and older gentlemen formally dressed with snow-white handkerchiefs in their breast pockets, constant chatter, and exchange of opinions; the usual background for social events of this kind. The following day, the pianist, his wife, and the manager who hadn't left their side, would return to Paris. Daniel would have a small reprieve there, and then he would continue his tour in the greatest concert halls of the world.

She avoided looking him in the eyes. She only lost her determination when it was time for them to leave, a bit earlier than the other guests, as was expected, and she couldn't avoid the eyes that hadn't stopped following her for the last three days.

A look can be even more powerful than a hug.

Part Three

Scherzando

The next few months went by in constant waiting. Not even she knew what she was waiting for. She devoted herself to charity work. That is what she knew best. She even finished reading two bulky novels, one of her favourite pastimes from when she was a young girl.

And she started reading the poems of Constantine P. Cavafy once more.

E su nel cielo è scritto:
Non ti vedrò mai più!

She received the same telegraph every week for six months.

Six months, and then nothing. For as many months. Perhaps even more. Perhaps an eternity. But, she had learned to wait.

Until this morning when the phone rang as soon as she entered the house. She quickly took off the gloves she was wearing to pick it up.

It was her sister.

It had been months since she had last contacted Daphne – nothing out of the ordinary.

Angela had just sent a few wishing cards for a couple of major holidays and had called only that one time when Daphne's daughter graduated from university. Vasia was her aunt's favourite because they were so much alike.

After they exchanged the usual greetings, Angela made her triumphant announcement with a carefree laugh – her famous laugh.

'I'm ready to immigrate to America, sweetie! A great star is born! I'll stay by his side forever. My darling needs me so much...

'I don't think I've mentioned it... Daniel and I split up.'

And as Daphne made no response, her sister continued talking.

'Pull yourself together, Laura! Isn't that what Daniel called you? Life waits for no one, darling!'

Then she laughed out loud again.

'I'm talking about something that concerns you. Haven't you been listening?'

'What?' Daphne stuttered. 'What can I say?'

'Don't act so surprised! It's not that big of a deal. It's just that... we had grown apart these last few months since our visit to Athens. Do you remember?'

Her sister was asking her if she remembered...

Angela continued talking, slightly out of breath.

'Since then, things changed. I don't know what went wrong. Then, I met Gerard, the joy of my life. And don't ask me how old he is.' Her all-too-familiar laugh followed. 'Age doesn't matter. Love is not about mathematical calculations. It just happens. I will invite you to New York soon. I won't take no for an answer. You will definitely come and bring my niece with you too. I'll be waiting to see you both.'

Daphne placed the handset back in its cradle. Her legs were shaking. She leaned against the small table nearby and then sat in the chair next to it.

She had the telegram she had received from him that morning clasped in her hand.

The sun slipped in through the window and bathed her in light.

She had surrendered herself to the music.

And he, the man who set the tempo and shaped the music, delivered the melody to her soul.

He was playing only for her. There was an endless, long discourse between them. Eternal and transient.

A discourse full of passion and intensity, full of memories and dreams.

And time was just another dimension. Her present was a musical vastness. A chimera of nothingness. A timeless intoxication. An eternal anticipation.

And her whole life had become a concerto for piano and orchestra.

Author's Note: The Italian verses that have been used as a title in three chapters of this book come from Giuseppe Verdi's opera *The Power of Destiny* (*La Forza del Destino*) and, more specifically, from Leonora's aria in Act IV.

Aphrodite Mermiga-Vlachaki was born in Athens. She is a graduate of the Ursuline Franco-Hellenic School and the Department of Medieval and Modern Greek Studies of the University of Athens, while she also has a degree in music in piano playing from the Athens Conservatoire.

She gave piano lessons in a private music school for a short period of time, before being appointed a philologist in the Arsakeion-Tositseion Schools, where she still teaches. She has been an active supporter of cultural events in the field of education by organizing performances in student theatrical festivals, rhetorical debates, and school events, adapting and directing theatrical plays, and providing music coordination.

In 2011, her first novel under the title *Και στη Ρώμη υπάρχει καλοκαίρι* [*There is Summer in Rome Too*] was published in Greece, followed by the publication of her novella *Daphne* in 2014; both by CaptainBook.gr Publishing.

Her poems have been featured in published poetry collections, while her poem *Lì ti ho visto* won an award in the international poetry contest Premio Accademico Internazionale di Poesia e Arte Contemporanea *Apollo dionisiaco* in 2015, Rome.

She is married with two children: a son and a daughter.